SHIP IN A BOTTLE

ANDREW PRAHIN

putnam

G. P. PUTNAM'S SONS

For Kathryn

G. P. PUTNAM'S SONS
An imprint of Penguin Random House LLC, New York

Copyright © 2021 by Andrew Prahin

G. P. Putnam's Sons is a registered trademark of Penguin Random House LLC.

Visit us online at penguinrandomhouse.com

Library of Congress Cataloging-in-Publication Data
Names: Prahin, Andrew, author, illustrator.
Title: Ship in a bottle / Andrew Prahin.
Description: New York: G. P. Putnam's Sons, [2021] | Summary: Mouse lives in constant fear of the cat and
is searching for a better life, so she sets off in her ship in a bottle to look for a new home.
Identifiers: LCCN 2020034118 (print) | LCCN 2020034119 (ebook) | ISBN 9781984815811 (hardcover) | ISBN 9781984815828 (epub) |
ISBN 9781984815835 (kindle edition)
Subjects: CYAC: Mice—Fiction. | Animals—Fiction. | Ship models in bottles—Fiction.
Classification: LCC PZ7.P88646 Sh 2021 (print) | LCC PZ7.P88646 (ebook) | DDC [E]—dc23
LC record available at https://lccn.loc.gov/2020034118
LC ebook record available at https://lccn.loc.gov/2020034119

Manufactured in China by RR Donnelley Asia Printing Solutions Ltd.
ISBN 9781984815811
1 3 5 7 9 10 8 6 4 2

Design by Marikka Tamura
Text set in Cooper Lt BT
The art was done in pencil on paper, with color added digitally.

Mouse and Cat lived together.
But there were problems.

Mouse wanted to eat gingersnaps.

Cat wanted to eat Mouse.

Mouse wanted to enjoy the ship in a bottle.

Cat wanted to eat Mouse.

Mouse wanted to lie in the sun.

Cat wanted to lie in the sun.

And eat Mouse.

Mouse dreamed of a better life.

So Mouse filled the bottle with gingersnaps, said her goodbyes . . .

and pushed off.

Mouse sailed peacefully down the quiet river.

Her new life was off to an exceptionally pleasant start.

But then there were seagulls.
Rude, grabby seagulls.

Mouse dove deep into the bottle as the birds
fought to get at the gingersnaps inside.

Eventually, the seagulls tumbled away,
scrapping over the single stolen treat.

Mouse cautiously returned to the top of the bottle.
This time, she left the gingersnaps inside.

That evening, the little vessel floated toward the bank of a rich, rolling pasture.

As the bottle bumped ashore,
Mouse imagined making a snug
little home in the stone walls above.

And here was a friend to make.
Mouse offered her new friend a gingersnap.
The rabbit loved gingersnaps.

More friends arrived.
They, too, loved gingersnaps.

But when all the gingersnaps were gone, the rabbits
decided it was time for Mouse to move on.

Left with nothing but a few crumbs, Mouse drifted downstream for another day or two.

Eventually, even the crumbs ran out.
Mouse's stomach rumbled.
The sky rumbled back.

rumble RUMBLE!

Then, with a shock of lightning, a terrible storm arrived.
The ship in a bottle was tossed roughly between the waves.

Mouse frantically tore the sails from the ship . . .

and stuffed them into the bottle's opening.

Then she hung on with all her strength.

When the storm finally grumbled away,
Mouse found herself in an enormous city.

Near dawn, Mouse looked out upon an expanse of quiet trees and grass nestled among the towering buildings.

She removed the rudder from the back of her ship and paddled.

Mouse was awfully tired when she reached the shore.
As she climbed down from the bottle, a chipmunk appeared.

Mouse drew herself up nice and tall.
"I don't have any gingersnaps," she said.
Her stomach rumbled.

The rain returned, and the chipmunk left.

But the chipmunk came back.

And he brought a gift.

In the days that followed, Mouse met all sorts of new friends.
She helped them.

And they helped her.

There were no gingersnaps in her new home, but Mouse discovered french fries when some very nice seagulls invited her to dinner.

She continued to enjoy the ship in a bottle, usually with a few neighbors.

And whenever the sun's rays warmed the ground, Mouse would find a tidy little spot of her own and stretch out, without a care in the world.